HYPOCHONDRIA

Hypochondria

SARAH R. NEW

Book Cover by Sarah R. New using Canva

First Printing, 2026

ISBN: 978-1-9194759-0-5

Prologue

'Dear Ms Emma Susanna Rayburn,

You have recently had genetic testing for inherited mutations in the BRCA 1 and 2 genes, which are genes linked to the development of breast cancers. We are saddened to tell you that you have tested positive for these genes, and we would advise you to contact your doctor in order to discuss these results. At this appointment, pre-emptive treatment and further steps can be discussed.

We hope you find this information useful.

Sincerely,

Dr Erin Kain

***

Emma breathed out shakily as she read the letter. She had known it all along, deep down. She should never have put the testing off. her mother would have been furious with her, but she had been so, so scared.

“Be brave, Emma.” she muttered to herself, placing the letter down, and walking into the small galley kitchen to make a cup of tea. A cup of tea would make her feel better, she told herself.

And it also gave her five minutes to figure out what she wanted to do. She had to tell Jon, but before she told Jon, she needed to have a plan. She knew he would be upset at this. He always struggled when she was sick. Holly said that she thought he was mean when he was sick, but Emma knew that he just struggled seeing her in pain.

But this wasn’t being sick, right? This genetic testing was pre-emptive. It was meant to work out if she could get sick, if she could also develop the awful disease her mum had died of. And now, she knew the answer, but she also knew that there were treatment options available. That was good, right?

She couldn’t tell Jon.

Her heart sank as she stared into the cup of tea, the teabag swirling around and around, the tea getting stronger and stronger. How could she tell him? She had nothing to tell at this point. No plan, no treatment, no answers.

No, she decided. She would go to the appointment, she would get all the answers, and then she’d tell him. That would work, she decided. That would work.

Chapter One

Emma could not believe how well the village fete was going. Everywhere she looked, children were laughing and playing, people were milling about, chatting. The sun was shining down on the large field, filled with stalls and games and people just having a good time. The event had gone off spectacularly.

Annette Rayburn was a thing of wonder, Emma mused to herself as she watched her mother man the duck pond stall, ice cream, of course, in hand. The annual village fete Annette organised was always a success, but this one... this one had been her piece de resistance. This year, anything Annette seemed to touch turned into gold, but Emma didn't know why she was surprised. It had been her mother's twelfth year running this. She was a dab hand at this now, and she'd been showing Emma the ropes. Hopefully she could run this fete half as well as her mum could, one day.

This year was easily Annette's best. Gingham covered stalls were packed onto the field, selling all sorts of things from local artisans; cakes, pastries, cheeses. There were also artists and local makers stalls dotted in there. Emma would already be leaving with a beautiful canvas landscape for the living room, an intricately made leather bag and a significantly lighter purse.

The local florist was handing out blooms to anyone who would take one. Emma's old schoolmate was painting animals on children's faces, and somehow, Annette had browbeat a local carnival company into lending games and rides for the day. Emma could hear children shrieking in joy as they hurtled down the helter skelter, and couldn't stop a smile from pulling at the corners of her mouth.

She didn't see her mum walk over to her, two ice creams in hand, until Annette softly bumped her shoulder to hers, laughing at Emma's jump. She laughed loudly, ignoring Emma's scarlet cheeks.

"Off with the fairies again?" Annette asked through chuckles, handing her a flake 99. Emma smiled as she saw the raspberry sauce covering the ice cream. Her favourite.

"I was just thinking about how well this year's fete has gone." Emma murmured, seeing her mother beam with pride.

"Oh, yeah. Kinda proud of it." Annette grinned widely, but as Emma looked at her, she noticed the grin faded quickly.

"Everything alright?" Emma asked. Annette's face was blank now, and it worried Emma. Annette was always bright and excited, smiling... this sudden change in demeanour was scaring her.

"Mum?" She went to grab Annette's arm, but she seemed to shake out of it.

"Yeah, I'm fine. Eat your ice cream before it melts, you know it's over £2 each now? What a rip off." Annette chuckled before returning to her own ice cream, but Emma was now certain something was wrong.

"Mum, what's wrong. ...You know you can talk to me, right?" Emma asked anxiously, aware that she could hear the concern in her own voice. She might be 25, but she still felt like a little girl asking these questions, worrying she was bothering her mum, scared she was going to get shouted at. Annette sighed, and Emma recoiled, her intestines churning. She moved her gaze directly to her now melting ice cream.

"I wasn't going to tell you this here, but I guess you already must know. I bet Father Gerald's already running his mouth." Annette laughed, but it was forced and wooden. Her demeanour seemed to change almost instantly; shoulders sagged, mouth downturned, suddenly the greys in her hair and the wrinkles on her face seemed somehow suddenly more pronounced.

"I'm, er... not doing the village fete next year. This was my last one, so I really wanted to it go well. And it has! It's done fantastically! But, um, I'm going to miss it." Annette's gaze seemed to mist over as she spoke, not to Emma, but more to the air in front of her.

"Why not?" Was all Emma could ask, and it seemed to break the trance Annette had fallen into, as her head snapped to face Emma's. Emma realised she was searching for reassurance, as if she was still a young girl, but when her eyes met Annette's, all she felt was fear. Annette's eyes were soft, and loving, and filled with uncertainty.

"You love doing the fete." Emma continued, her voice fearful and shaky. "You don't have to give it up, you don't have to end it all on a high-"

"Oh, my girl." Annette cooed. "Sometimes things just have to change. We might not want them to, but sometimes they have to."

"But why?" Emma was aware that she sounded childish and petulant, but she couldn't stop herself.

"Because I'm sick, Emma." Annette started, taking a second to compose herself, before carrying on. "I got the results back from my mammogram a week or so ago, and it confirmed what my doctor and I thought. They said that it's breast cancer."

Emma thought that her mother probably kept talking, but she couldn't hear anything else. Breast cancer. How could that be? Her mum had always been so healthy! She had never smoked, hardly drank. She did everything she was supposed to. How could she be sick?

...How serious was it?

Panicked, Emma looked back at her mother, it finally dawning on her that her mother was crying. She couldn't even get the words out before her mother answered the question that was on the tip on her tongue.

"They said it's stage four." Annette whispered.

And that's when everything changed.

Chapter Two

Emma tried so hard not to think about the last time she was here. The waiting room hadn't changed; still the same pale yellow on the walls, same battered wooden furniture, even the same magazines available to read. It was like nothing had changed, but everything had changed in the last eighteen months. It made her head spin.

She wished she had told Jon, or her best friend Holly, or anyone. She wished she hadn't come here alone. She wished she had someone to hold her hand.

"Emma Rayburn?" she heard, and she turned to see a young doctor smiling at her. Emma tried to smile back, but she felt her smile falter. She had expected Dr Mogfield. She had asked for him specifically, remembering how good he had been with her mother. This young, fresh faced, female doctor was not Dr Mogfield.

"Yes?" She replied hesitantly, hoping that she would take her to Dr Mogfield. Already, she could hear the anxious thoughts swirling around and around in her mind. *This woman doesn't know you, doesn't know your history, she can't help you. You should leave.*

"Ms Rayburn? We should start the appointment. Please follow me." The doctor gestured as she started to walk away. With every cell of her body screaming against it, Emma found herself standing up and following her. The appointment room was only a few steps down the hall, but Emma found her legs getting heavier and heavier as she walked, her breath getting shakier and shakier, her hands feeling tickly and numb...

"Please sit down." The doctor indicated with a nod and a smile. Emma obeyed instinctively, watching as the doctor sat on the other side of the desk. Was this the same appointment room she had been in before, with her mum? She couldn't tell. Hospital rooms all looked the same after a while.

"So, I'm Dr Erin Kain, I work with Dr Mogfield. I'll be taking your case from now on." She said brightly.

"W...why isn't Dr Mogfield taking my case?" Emma asked, her voice shaky. Dr Kain smiled. Emma could tell that she was trying to be reassuring, but she felt like the doctor was being patronising.

"Dr Mogfield is currently taking a step back from new cases, but will consult if needed, but to be completely honest with you, Ms Rayburn, I really don't think it'll be a problem." Dr Kain smiled again, her voice warm, but all Emma could think about was the anxiety swirling around and around in her mind.

"But why is Dr Mogfield taking a step back?" She continued, noticing that the smile on Dr Kain's face seemed somewhat strained.

"I believe it's due to family matters. I do think we should move on to the results of the genetic testing, that is what you're here for, yes?" Dr Kain continued. Emma nodded, and she looked down at her notes.

"So, I can see here that you've been tested for the BRCA 1 and 2 genes due to your mother testing positive for them, correct?" Dr Kain asked. Emma nodded.

"And your mother is being treated for breast cancer?" Dr Kain asked. Emma took a deep breath, willing the tears not to come.

"She was. She died about a year ago. From the cancer." Emma murmured. Dr Kain's face fell.

"I'm so sorry for your loss." It seemed sincere to Emma, but then the doctor immediately moved on.

"I see here that you've also tested positive for these genes. Have you noticed anything different about your chest area at all? Any lumps, or irregularities you're concerned about?" She asked, and Emma shook her head.

"No, nothing at all." It was a slight lie. That morning, Emma had noticed a slight bump under the skin of her armpit, but she didn't want to think about it. She decided that it was a cyst. It couldn't be cancer. She couldn't let it be cancer.

She could tell Dr Kain didn't believe her, judging by the sceptical look on her face, but she continued.

"We will offer regular breast cancer screenings immediately from now on, so that means mammograms and MRI scans.

There are also other options, for instance we can offer preventative medicines, risk-reducing surgeries, or many people simply ask for our support whilst making lifestyle choices..." Dr Kain kept talking, but Emma was trapped inside her mind again.

She's brought up breast cancer several times now. Does that mean I'm more likely to get breast cancer? I must do, because of Mum. And if I am more likely to get it, lifestyle changes aren't doing to help me. Mum tried that at first, it didn't work. No, I can't have cancer. It'll kill me. There's only one option.

Dr Kain was still talking, but Emma couldn't wait, blurting out her question.

"When you say risk-reducing surgery, do you mean a mastectomy?" Emma couldn't get the words out fast enough, noticing how Dr Kain's face softened with pity.

"Yes, and also a possible hysterectomy, if needed. I have some pamphlets here with information that you can take away and read-"

"How much will my risk of cancer be reduced by? If I have the mastectomy?" Emma asked. She could hear the panic in her own voice. Judging by the concern on her face, Dr Kain could hear it as well.

"Up to 50%, but there's no guara-"

"I want the mastectomy. And the hysterectomy as well. Can we do them at the same time?" Emma asked, unable to get the words out fast enough. Her hands were shaky, she could feel herself sweaty, but she knew she needed this. She couldn't have cancer. She couldn't have cancer. She couldn't have cancer.

Staring at Dr Kain's incredulous face, Emma could feel that Dr Kain wasn't going to agree, but she so, so needed her too. If she didn't get the approval, cancer would consume her from the inside out, she knew it. Just like her mother, her distrustful inner voice echoed in her mind. And her mother had died in such pain, with no dignity. No, Emma couldn't let that happen to her. She stared deep at Dr Kain, hoping, pleading mentally to her, praying that she would understand why Emma was asking, hoping she would realise that this mastectomy would save her.

Dr Kain sighed.

"How about we do the mastectomy, and then once you've recovered and we've done some tests, we talk about a hysterectomy?" She asked. Emma smiled, feeling like a balloon slowly deflating after being overinflated for way too long.

"Deal." Emma agreed, elated.

Chapter Three

Emma stared at the two cups of tea in front of her. The steam that had been billowing when she had poured it had now slowed, and she shook her head, trying to bring herself back to normality as she reached for the biscuits. Custard creams, Mum's favourite. Hopefully she'd eat these. Emma picked up the tray to walk into the living room.

Normality. What wouldn't Emma give to go back to the normality of last year, when she had her own little place and she hadn't had to move home and Mum wasn't sick. She'd do anything for Mum not to be sick.

Carefully, she pushed open the door to the living room, wincing as the door trailed over the thick carpet, hoping she hadn't woken Mum. Emma had drawn the curtains almost permanently since the hospital bed had been moved in here, but the sunshine yellow room always reflected light, and Emma was sure that it must be hard to try and sleep. She had offered to get blackout blinds for the room, but her mother had refused, stating that she liked the colour and wanted to see it properly. And Emma couldn't argue with her Mum, not now. Emma crept into the room, noticing her mother prone in the bed and placed the tray down quickly. Her heart quickened. *Not now, not now,* she thought. She had just been out of the room for a moment! She ran over to her, arm overstretched to check her pulse...

"Boo!" Her mother shouted, and Emma jumped back from shock. Heart pounding, breath caught in her throat, tears in her eyes, she suddenly felt a huge wave of anger come over her.

"That's not funny!" She shouted; teeth bared as if she were facing an enemy. It felt like she was, in a way. Her mother had been bright and funny and vibrant, once upon a time. Before the lump. Before the biopsy. Before the cancer. The cancer, ravaging her mother's body, pushing her closer and closer to the precipice of death, and her mother, once a warrior but now a willing participant, laughing her way closer and closer to the end. Her mother's face crumpled slightly at Emma's shout, and then softened.

"I'm sorry, honey." She cooed, opening her arms to Emma. "I didn't mean to scare you." Automatically, Emma walked over to her, leaning into her once warm and comforting embrace.

Annette was still her mother, of course, but she was changed. Months of chemo and radiation had indelibly warped her body. Her eyes were still kind, but almost all her flesh had been seared away from her bones, leaving her skeletal. She had become weak and unable to care for herself, so of course Emma had left her life in London to move back home and look after her. It felt like a weird role reversal for Emma, but her mother seemed quite content to have her home. Annette had found comfort in loud headscarves and patterned prints, but all Emma could see when she was displaying them was the increasing paleness and crepe like texture of her mother's skin.

"It's not funny," Emma attempted to scold, but her voice just sounded petulant and pouty, especially when she was curled in her mother's arms.

"It's a little bit funny." Annette laughed a little, but it seemed to catch in the back of her throat, and she started coughing. Immediately, Emma jumped up, grabbing the closest bottle with drinkable water in and trying to force it into Annette's mouth.

"I'm fine, I'm fine, Emma!" Annette pushed her away, rubbing at her chest. Emma stared at her, so frail, so ...different to whoever she had ever been before. Finally, the coughing subsided, and Annette smiled weakly at her.

"I think I might try to have a nap, honey." Annette smiled, but Emma knew what she meant. She was being dismissed. She turned and started walking out of the room.

"I'll wake you in a couple of hours." She tried to smile as she said it, pushing down the tears that were steadily making their way to her eyes. As she closed the door, she caught sight of the two cups of tea she had left on the side, surely stone cold by now.

Chapter Four

Emma did not know how to tell Jon. In fact, she would rather not tell Jon at all, but she knew that wasn't an option. Especially now.

Holding the letter in her hand, her heart skipped a beat when she read the operation date. 10th May 2024. Barely a month away. Not even a month, and then she could relax. She'd be safe. She'd be safe.

But Jon was going to be furious, and Emma didn't know how she was going to soften the blow. She didn't know if she wanted to. She didn't want him to try and talk her out of it.

In the recesses of her mind, she heard the front door close with a SLAM! She let out a long, grounding sigh, and plastered a fake smile on her face in anticipation. Jon was home.

He walked into the bedroom, throwing his jacket on the bed, kicking off his shoes, not a word spoken to her. Rage seemed to radiate from him.

"You alright?" Emma tried, noticing that she had automatically raised the pitch of her voice, scrunched herself down to make herself smaller, anything not to set him off. Gently, she folded the letter, placing it on her bedside table. Jon didn't even look at her as he walked into the bathroom, slamming that door behind him as well. She didn't even flinch, just let out a small sigh of frustration. She'd tell him later.

***

Emma: i got the letter today

Gemma: what letter?

Sammy: omg you did?

Holly: Em!!! this is fantastic!

Gemma: what letter?

Emma: the one from the hospital

Sammy: the one about the mastectomy, right? or are they making you do treatment before?

Holly: is it soon?

Emma: 10th May

Holly: 10th May! that's so soon!

Gemma: a mastectomy? isn't that a bit drastic?

Sammy: are they gonna give you new boobs? do you get to choose the size?

Holly: this is such good news babe! it's gonna be such a weight off your shoulders once its gone

Sammy: *weight off your boobs

"Who are you texting?" Jon spat as Emma quickly muted her phone, not realising how loud the text alert actually was. They had decided to go to bed a while ago, until Jon had realised that Fulham were playing and absolutely had to watch it. All Emma had wanted to do was go to sleep, but that wasn't happening for hours yet.

"Just the girls." She replied, trying to sound nonchalant. The football match Jon was watching was significantly louder, but she couldn't be bothered to argue the point.

"Well, can you ever mute it or shut up? I'm watching the game." He snapped.

"Can't you hear it well enough?" she muttered underneath her breath, not realising he was still looking at her.

"What was that?" His voice got louder and louder, angrier and angrier. She didn't want to deal with this.

"I said I'm gonna sleep on the sofa, I'm tired." She lied through her teeth, not even blinking at how easy it was. Quickly, she exited the bed and headed towards the door, not noticing her quick movement had caused the letter to flutter from the bedside table to the floor. She was nearly out of the door when she heard it.

"What's that?"

She turned around to see Jon reading the letter, his face darkening and darkening the further down the letter he read.

"What does this mean, mastectomy?" He was shouting, spit flying from his mouth. "What the fuck aren't you telling me?" She hadn't even noticed the tears falling down her face.

"I tested positive for the BRCA genes, and I am having the mastectomy as preventative treatment." Her voice was shaky but clear, and she found her hands curled into fists as she had to explain herself. *How dare he not support her? How dare he act like this? It was like he wanted her sick,* was circling around and around in her mind.

"Without even saying anything?" He rebutted, not as loud this time. She noticed that he seemed to be getting paler and quieter rather than angrier. She didn't care.

"Well, it's not your decision, is it, Jon? Either you're here for the surgery on the 10th, or you're not. I don't even care either which way." She spat at him, slamming the door behind her as she ran down the stairs, hands gripping at her mouth to stifle her cries.

***

Blink. Blink. Emma's sight was hazy and her eyes heavy as she came around from the anaesthesia but that didn't matter. She was elated. The danger was gone. Slowly, carefully, she raised her hand and went to touch her chest, but a firm hand around her wrist stopped her.

"Careful, Emma, it's going to be very sore." Dr Kain warned, smiling down at her.

"Was it cool? I feel like the operation was cool." Emma asked, her words slurred. She physically couldn't feel anything but emotionally, she was on top of the world. Dr Kain chuckled, letting go of Emma's wrist.

"It went really well. We got everything, we're very confident in the margins we've left, and it was really, really cool." Dr Kain's grin matched Emma's emerging one. "Now, please, rest. We'll come around with the results in a day or so."

"Thank you, Doctor." A gruff reply came from beside her as Dr Kain left the room. Surprised, Emma turned her head, surprised to see Jon sitting next to her.

"You're here?" She asked, heart leaping. He shook his head.

"Yeah?" There was a sting in his voice, but Emma didn't pick up on it as she closed her eyes and sunk into the pain medication.

Chapter Five

She should have just ordered a cab, Emma lectured herself, as she finally managed to dump the bags in the hallway. Eight bags for life full of groceries! She was surprised she had managed the 20 minute walk home.

She made sure to lock the door behind her, shaking out her aching hands as she did. She hoped the throbbing would stop soon. Carefully, taking the bags two at a time this time, Emma moved the bags into the kitchen. She didn't bother about being quiet. She was pretty sure she would have woken Mum up trying just to get into the house.

Emma started unpacking all of the bags and sorting out where everything had to go when she heard a 'tsk' from the doorframe behind her. She turned, already knowing who it was. Standing in the doorway, an impeccably dressed woman in her 60s, the most glamorous person she knew. The woman who had helped raise her.

"Auntie Lisa!" Emma squealed, running to envelope her in a hug.

"Hello, darling." Lisa smiled, her arms hanging loosely around Emma. "It's been a while."

"You've been away." Emma mumbled into her shoulder. Lisa patted her back hesitantly.

"I'm back now," Lisa confirmed.

"How long for?" Emma asked as they parted. Lisa shook her head.

"As long as I need to be. I guess." She sounded unsure. Emma didn't feel completely satisfied with the answer, but it would work for now, she decided. If Lisa wanted to stay and help, Emma wasn't going to stop her. She could use the help.

"Is Mum awake?" She asked, already wincing at the question. With how noisy she had been dragging the bags in, there was almost no chance she was still asleep. Lisa shot her a look.

"You know she is, young miss, after that racket you made in the hallway! Hurry up and get everything away, I'll make a cup of tea, and your mum can tell you about this god-awful film she just made me watch." Lisa remarked and Emma snorted.

"If it's the one I'm thinking of, she's watched it every day for the last fortnight." Emma laughed. Lisa's face dropped.

"Really?" she exclaimed. "Jesus Christ, I thought she had better taste than that." Lisa walked out of the kitchen, Emma's giggles following her.

Chapter Six

Emma's head pounded as Gemma shrieked in laughter, over and over. She had been at home for nearly three days now, and the pain medication was just not hitting as hard as it had been. Jon wasn't at home, of course. He had claimed that he needed to stay closer to work for the week, stating that it was a big week at work, but they both knew the real reason. He hadn't looked her in the eye since the operation, had hardly spoken to her. She didn't really care. She'd lost all respect for him anyway.

But she still had her girls. The minute she had told them the date of the operation, her best friend Holly had dropped everything to be there, by her side. And once one of them came, Sammy and Gemma had trailed along, asking all sorts of personal, embarrassing questions. But she loved them all for it.

And now it was three days later, and she was exhausted by the late-night girly wine chats Sammy and Gemma had insisted on, and the lack of consistent pain medication and the constant ache all across her chest. She could barely move her arms, couldn't reach for anything. It hurt All. The. Time. and the incessant giggle-shrieking and shit-talking from Sammy and Gemma. It was exhausting, having to host all the time while being sick, and she didn't think she could do it anymore. She found herself, along with Holly, holed up in her bedroom, while Sammy and Gemma spent the nights dancing away, music cranked to maximum on someone's phone, drinking all the alcohol Emma had in the house.

She'd had enough. She was done.

"Maybe I need to tell them to leave." She mused out loud, as Holly softly stroked her hair.

"You shouldn't have to do that." Holly murmured back. And Emma knew that she was right, but her head was pounding and she was in so much pain.

"But I can't go on like this." She moaned. She could cry. She had to do something. Pulling herself to her feet, she walked to the door and opened it, firmly, like she was on a mission. She was, in a way. She knew what she needed to do, and somehow, that knowledge was starting to make her feel better.

She gingerly made her way down the staircase, Holly close on her heels, feeling more and more energetic as she went. She could hear Holly protesting behind her, but she almost couldn't hear what she was saying. She wouldn't admit it to her, but she really didn't care what Holly was saying. She knew what she needed to do.

Finally at the bottom of the staircase, she grabbed the door handle and entered the living room, letting the words blurt out before she even took in what was going on in the room.

"Gemma, Sammy, I love you both, but I'm done. I'm sorry. I really appreciate you both coming over to help me, but I think you're using this more of a girls' trip rather than helping me out and I appreciate you coming, of course I do, but... I need to rest, and this isn't helping, so I love you both, but, please, both of you, leave." Emma blurted out, feeling an almost immediate relief when the words got off her chest, but then she looked around and that sinking feeling crashed back into her. Sammy and Gemma were holed up in the living room, like she thought, and the room looked like a bomb site, like she expected, but they weren't alone. Jon was standing next to Gemma, his hand brushing her arm, as if he was going to grab her hand. Emma found herself taking a short, sharp breath in. She didn't know how to feel.

"You're chucking us out?" Sammy asked, teeth bared the way she always did any time she felt slightly threatened. Emma almost wished she didn't feel that way, but she was also mad. *How dare she feel like that after acting like this towards Emma in her own house?*

"I just need some space. Thank you, both, for coming." Emma reiterated, her voice firm. This was the thing she had felt most sure about for weeks, and she wasn't going to let them stop her.

"Bit harsh, don't you think, Em?" Jon interrupted, his hands in his pockets as he stared at her. Emma stared him down, unwilling to bend this time. She was in pain, she was tired and she hated that fucking nickname.

"I'm going to bed." She announced. "Let them out, won't you, Jon?" She didn't wait for an answer as she turned to make her way back up the staircase.

Chapter Seven

"So we did find some pre-cancerous cells in the breast tissue we extracted from you, however, it was a very small area, and the fact that they were pre-cancerous doesn't mean that there was actual cancer there, but it could have turned into cancer, so it's great that we caught it so early. All the tests we've done today look good, however. Obviously, we'll keep an eye on you, we'll do some tests in a few months, but I think this proves that you made the right decision in going for the mastectomy." Dr Kain looked relieved as she delivered the news. In the back of her mind, Emma wondered if she was relieved that they had found the pre-cancerous cells. Did it make it all worth it?

It made it all seem worth it to Emma.

"Thank you, doctor." Emma replied, almost on autopilot, grasping the piece of paper that had her test results on it. She couldn't wait until she got home, and could look Jon in the face and say 'see! I told you I needed the surgery!'

She probably wouldn't actually do it, but it was the thought that counted. Carefully tucking the letter into her bag, she smiled, a weight she didn't know was hanging around her shoulders suddenly being lifted.

***

Emma bounded through the front door, feeling lighter than she had done in a year. God, it's been over a year, she thought to herself as she carefully locked the door behind her. A year since Mum. Emma wondered whether her mum would be proud of her.

The house seemed messier than it did when she left, but she tried not to let it bother her as she made her way into the kitchen, looking for Jon. She looked around the door. The kitchen was a bombsite, dishes unwashed from breakfast and seemingly lunch, piled in the sink, rubbish scattered on the floor. She'd be cleaning that up later, she thought to herself.

The living room door was open, and she could see that that room was completely empty, so Emma made her way upstairs. *He's probably having a nap*, she thought to himself. *He was out late last night.* But as she inched closer and closer to the bedroom door, she could hear the telltale signs of gunfire and screaming. He was gaming. She rolled her eyes before opening the door.

He was laying on the bed, clad in only his underwear and an old, holey shirt, surrounded by snacks and glazed over, staring at the television screen. He didn't even look at her as she walked in. Irritation flared in her temple as she looked at all the crumbs and smears of chocolate on her previously pristine bedsheets, but she didn't want to let him ruin this moment.

"Jon!" She trilled, almost bouncing with excitement. She couldn't calm down. The feeling of vindication, of knowing she was right and had been all along, was too strong.

He didn't look at her. She continued.

"I just got back to the doctors and they said that they did find some cells that would have turned into cancer, but that they managed to catch them in time! And all my other tests went really well, they said I'm doing so well and that I made the right decision and can go back to work next week!" She concluded, holding out the letter to show him. He didn't even look over at it, or her. She pretended like it wasn't hurt, but it did, it did, it did.

"Was it worth it?" Were the only words that spilt from his disinterested mouth, his eyes not leaving the screen. It felt like a gut punch to Emma.

"What?" She asked, her voice shaky, as he lay there, on her bed, ignoring her. This was her house, her mother's house, and he couldn't even look at her?

"Was it worth having your boobs chopped off? I mean, look at you. You've mutilated yourself, make it hard for me to look at you at all. No other man's gonna want you. Was it worth it?" He asked, boredom in his voice, still refusing to look at her. Emma's eyes filled with tears, but she wasn't upset, no, she was angry, furious with him. She hated him.

"I hate you." She whispered, choking on the words as she tried to get them out. If he heard her, which she doubted he did, he didn't react, still staring at his off brand, generic, shooting game, still worming his crumbs into her safe bed, still pushing her out of the one place that was supposed to be hers.

Chapter Eight

Emma had always hated hospitals.

She could never place why, but even setting foot in a hospital made her feel sick. She thought that maybe it was the smell. That bleachy, antisepticy smell that you never smell anywhere else, just so hospital specific. It always made her feel like she was going to throw up. Her mum would often say she developed the phobia as a child, when she broke her arm that one time on an empty stomach, and threw up the minute they tried to give her any pain killers.

Her mother had never had that problem though. Annette thrived in hospitals. In a way, it was second nature to her, being the caring person that she was. She was always organising charity events, sneaking sweets and toys into the paediatric wing, she'd even helped paint a mural in the lobby for the hospital. Even today, sitting in the oncology ward, Annette sat there happily flicking through the old, dated magazines. Her own arms tucked tightly around her; Emma nudged Annette.

"How are you okay with this?" She whispered. Annette flashed her the page of the magazine she was reading.

"I don't think anyone would be okay with a killer squirrel coming into their house and stealing their frozen peas." She chortled. Emma started at her, completely confused by her indifference. Annette leant over, softly lifting her chin.

"I know, the stealing of the peas shocked me as well. Surely that just makes it a thieving squirrel? Who did it kill?" She kept on, giggling mainly to herself.

"How are you laughing at a time like this? We're in the oncology ward! We're waiting for your results! How are you-" It was like the words could not stop themselves from falling out of Emma's mouth. Annette glared at her daughter.

"You need to calm down. This is a place people receive the worst news of their life, and you are not helping right now." Her voice was steady yet firm, and it made Emma want to burst into tears.

"Mum-" Emma started, teary, but Annette sternly placed her finger to her lips.

"Emma. Stop it. Now." Annette settled back in her chair, going back to her magazine, but she seemed different now, perturbed even. Emma hated the thought that she had done that to her.

***

The appointment room was even worse than the waiting room, Emma thought to herself. She sat there, legs jiggling uncontrollably, arms held tightly around herself as they waited for the doctor to come in. Annette, in her usual way, was sat there, looking around, completely calm.

"Emma, stop that, you'll make me nervous." Annette remarked, a little laugh in her voice. Emma ignored her.

"How can the doctor tell you to come in and then keep you waiting longer? That just seems unfair. Cruel, even." She ranted, and Annette snorted.

"Cruel? Wow, you do go on." Annette laughed.

"You know what I mean! He should have had all your tests and everything already printed and ready to go for when you got in here!" Emma reiterated, watching her mum roll her eyes at her. It irritated her more than she wanted to admit.

"Emma, it's really not a big deal. The oncologists are very busy, they have a lot of patients and it's not poor Dr Mogfield's fault that the printer's broken. You know what the NHS is like now days, there's no one with enough time or money to help him fix it. It'll just be a minute or two. You do go on sometimes." Annette tutted lovingly.

"I'm just saying-" Emma started, but the door opened, and she quickly leant back in her chair, trying not to give off that she had been complaining. Annette pulled a face at her, trying not to laugh at her daughter as an obviously flustered Dr Mogfield walked in. He was a short, grey haired man with a kindly face and thick lensed glasses. Annette had once said he reminded her of an overworked owl.

“I'm so sorry to keep you waiting.” He apologised, quickly shaking their hands as he sat down.

“It's not bother, please, take your time.” Annette smiled at him. The smile seemed to work, and he slowed slightly.

“So, Ms Rayburn, you're here today to pick up your latest test results, correct?” He asked, and Annette nodded.

“Yes, although I was hoping that the genetic tests would be back as well? I know that that's a long shot, as they were so recent, but I'd just like some piece of mind on my daughter's behalf.” She asked, a slight anxiety clear in her voice and Emma's face fell. Genetic tests? She didn't know anything about that.

“What?” she started, but Annette swatted at her as Dr Mogfield looked through the paperwork.

“Well, you're in luck, Ms Rayburn! I saw that they came in this morning, I was just getting them printed prior to the appointment. Figured the two of you would want to know.” He smiled. Annette smiled back at him.

“Thank you so much, doctor, that's so thoughtful.” She praised, and he looked genuinely surprised.

“Uh, no problem! So, getting into the results, you have tested positive for the BRCA genes 1 and 2, which means that is it likely your disease has developed due to these genes. Now, obviously, we don't know that for sure, it could be a weird coincidence, but I would recommend your daughter gets tested as well. That being said, it doesn't mean that you do have those genes, Miss Rayburn, but the testing can help with peace of mind and possible future planning." He concluded, and Annette nodded.

"Of course. I think that's a great idea. Are you happy to be put forward for that, Emma?" She asked. Emma's head was swimming. *BRCA genes... genetic disease ...future planning? She couldn't make sense of it.*

"I ...suppose so?" she answered, surprised by the words coming out of her mouth.

"Great! I'll get my colleague Dr Kain to contact you." Dr Mogfield nodded as he made a note. As he started flicking through the pages of results, his face darkened.

"Now, erm, Ms Rayburn, to move on to your other results..." he started, when Annette cut him off.

"It's okay doctor. I know what you're going to say." she stopped him. He looked confused.

"Did you get a second opinion?" he asked, confused, but Annette shook her head.

"No, no, I just ...have had a gut feeling about this for a while, and the look on your face there just confirmed it. But it's okay. It's okay, I'm okay with it, honestly. It feels like it was supposed to happen, in a way. I never really expected to live a long life, and I've had so much more than I expected." Annette was tearing up as she spoke, her hand reaching over to clutch Emma's. Emma's head was reeling. *What was happening? How did she know? Was she not prepared to fight, for herself, for Emma?*

"I don't want to know how long, or what it's going to be like or anything like that, I just needed to know, for certain. And now I do. Thank you, Dr Mogfield." Annette sighed, almost with relief. She stood up confidently, definitively.

"I wish you all the best, Ms Rayburn. Both of you." The doctor's voice was thick and heavy with tears as he leant forward to shake their hands, and Annette gracefully got up to usher Emma out of the room.

"Wait, no." Emma started, her head spinning. Her throat clenched. She was confused. Did this mean her mum was going to die? Could she not save her?

"It's okay, honey." Her mum, still crying, cooed, stroking her hair as she led her down the corridor. *No*, Emma thought, *no, this was wrong, this was all wrong.*

"Mum." She whispered, and Annette squeezed her hand.

"There's nothing that can be done." She whispered back, as she guided Emma to the exit. "There's nothing else that can be done."

Chapter Nine

"That's fantastic news!" Holly buzzed over the phone. "Does that mean you've got the all clear, or..."

"No, I'm going in next week for the all clear, hopefully. I'm really worried the tests are going to be wrong and will have mutated since they last checked." Emma admitted. She felt secure with Holly, like she could be completely vulnerable with her. Holly had been a great help since her mother's death, possibly the only person who had. Gemma and Sammy were sweet, but they really couldn't quite get the impact her mother's death had had on Emma. And she'd met Jon a few weeks after the funeral. Lisa hadn't approved of him, and they'd fought, and she hadn't spoken to her since. But Holly, Holly had always been there for her.

She debated for a couple of seconds whether to tell her about the fight her and Jon had had. Well, it wasn't exactly a fight, but Emma had felt badly about it. But something in the back of her mind stopped her. It seemed stupid, somehow, like it wasn't that bad. *She was overreacting, like normal*, she decided. *She just needed to stop*.

"Do you want me to come with you to the appointment?" Holly's voice cut through the swirling thoughts of Emma's mind, and her heart softened slightly at Holly's words.

"That's so sweet of you, but please don't worry. I'm going to be fine, the doctor basically just said it was something they had to check again to confirm everything. Don't worry. I'll let you know everything the minute I do, okay?" She said, brightly, hoping Holly couldn't hear the fear in her voice, or that she might burst into tears any minute.

"You better! Hey, I have to go back to work now, but you tell me everything, okay? I love you!" Holly joked, and Emma was surprised to feel her heart sink as she realised Holly had taken her completely seriously.

"Love you too." She managed to blurt out before the phone disconnected, and Emma realised how alone she really was.

***

"So, Emma, I can confirm that the tests all say that you have no active disease. You're cancer free! Congratulations!" Dr Kain beamed as she delivered the news, but Emma couldn't focus on anything other than the THUD THUD THUD of her heart. She should feel relieved, she knew that, but as she searched deep down in the recesses of her soul for that emotion, she couldn't find it. It was like it didn't exist.

You should be happy. Why aren't you happy? Wait, I know... It's because the doctor is wrong, isn't it? It's because you know, deep down, that something really is wrong with you. Let's face it, if it wasn't for your mother insisting that you get that test you would never have known about those pre-cancerous cells. Pre-cancerous. How close did you get to death, Emma? Do you even know? Can you even comprehend how easily you could have died? And what else is swirling around in that body of yours, under the surface where you can't see? Because there's almost definitely something else. These things don't happen in isolated incidents. If there's cancer, then you're almost definitely sick with something else. This is a reprieve, not an escape, that's for certain.

"Emma? This is good news! This means that everything you've gone through has been worth it." Dr Kain tried to reassure her, but Emma couldn't believe her. *Not everything has been worth it.*

The doctor stood up, still smiling, and ushered Emma to the door. Seemingly on autopilot, Emma smiled back, walking out of the door.

"Good luck!" Dr Kain called after her as Emma left, waving. *Good luck? That's a weird thing to say,* her traitorous brain mused, but Emma tried to shake the thought out as she left the oncology department, hoping with everything in her that she wouldn't have to come back here ever again.

***

Emma: just got the news. officially cancer free

Holly: OMG I CANT BELIEVE IT

Sammy: yay Emma!

Gemma: congrats

Holly: I KNEW YOU COULD BEAT IT

Gemma: well it wasn't like she actually had cancer.

Sammy: still! it's a really big achievement Em

Emma: thanks everyone

Holly: we should all go out and celebrate!

Sammy: omg yes! we definitely should

Gemma: we should defo go out! definitely out though so Em doesn't chuck us out for no reason again

Emma: well i don't even know if I want to go out

Gemma: stop being such a cow! we should all totes go out, and just not crash at Em's in case she's PMS'ing again

Sammy: gem you're so funny!

Holly: erm no she's not! Em was recovering from major surgery and you two were just making things awful for her!

Gemma: god, Holly, calm down it's just a joke

Sammy: wow you guys can't take a joke

Holly: you know what? maybe we won't all go out.

Sammy: wow!

Gemma: such an overreaction, Holls!

Holly: definitely isn't! Em's just gone through something awful and you two are being horrible to her and making it all about you!

Emma: i agree

Gemma: well of course you do, you two are basically joined at the hip, its like without the other, neither of you can have an original thought

Sammy: so funny, gem!

Gemma: let me tell you both what, we're both gonna go out tonight, and if you two can get your acts together and apologise, you can come with. see you later!

Gemma has left the chat.
Sammy has left the chat.

Holly: god, what a pair of arseholes! i'm so sorry, Em.

Emma: it's not your fault.

Holly: just, what an accomplishment and they've ruined it!

Emma: it's okay, Holls. It's not like i accomplished anything, really.

Holly: oh shut up! this is incredible

Emma: i just feel like this isn't over

Holly: it's gonna feel like that for a while, you're in shock! everything's gonna be fine!

Emma felt sick as she closed the text. She hoped that she was wrong, and that Holly was right and she was overreacting. God, she hoped Holly was right.

Chapter Ten

The mole on her arm had changed.

She knew it. She could tell. It was slight — very slight, almost imperceptible — but it was there. She could tell. The shape was different — less rounded, a slight dent at the bottom and a slight bump at the top, as if it was trying to move place — and it seemed browner than usual? She thought?

It's cancer again. Dr Kain knew it, and that's why she said good luck. She knew that it wasn't breast cancer, but skin cancer, and she just couldn't bear to tell you. You never got better, you were always sick.

She knew she was still sick.

"Emma!" She snapped back to reality at hearing Holly's voice, her mind spinning for a second. Where were they? She looked around, realising they were in Holly's favourite clothing shop, and that she was holding a dress against her body.

"Yeah?" She asked, completely unsure of what they were meant to be doing. She had no idea; she had been so focused on her mole... Holly was looking at her with concern written all over her face. God, she hated that.

"I'm fine, Holly." Emma stood up and smoothed down her dress, deliberately not looking at the mole. She knew Holly wouldn't buy it.

"You're staring at that mole again." Holly sighed. Emma felt herself flush red, wanted to disappear inside her clothes and shatter into atoms, but instead she just walked past Holly, grabbing her bag, making her way to the door.

"Are we going?" She asked, wincing at the impatience in her voice, and her heart sunk as she saw Holly try not to roll her eyes. She was already sick, she knew that, but she couldn't lose her best friend as well.

***

"I cannot believe you dragged us here!" Emma laughed as she grabbed onto an also giggling Holly's arm. Holly had been so insistent on going to this new club that Emma had finally given in and agreed to go. It had only been open a few months, but already it looked dingy and grimy, and the girls immediately decided they had to move on.

"I'm so sorry! I heard this place was great!" Holly apologised as they made their way to the exit.

"I can't believe they haven't even got an alcohol license!" Emma cackled, Holly laughing hard alongside her, grabbing her arm as if she couldn't hold herself up.

"We haven't even drank anything and you're acting drunk!" Emma pushed Holly, still laughing, when she realised Holly had stopped, straightened herself up and was staring across the road. Her face was stern, and angry, and the joy in Emma's heart started to die when she saw the seriousness that had come over her friend.

"What?" She asked, turning to see where Holly was looking. Holly seemed to snap out of her stare.

"Wait—" Holly started, but it was too late. Emma looked across the road, and saw Jon standing there, his hand in another woman's hair, his lips on another woman's. Emma felt her heart drop as he pulled away.

"Is that Gemma?" Rage rose through Emma and she found herself storming over to the couple. She could hear Holly's panicked footsteps behind her, but she could not—would not — stop.

"How dare you!" She screamed, grabbing at Jon's top and pulling them apart. She caught sight of Gemma's smug face and wanted to beat it right off of her face, but her body faced Jon, and the look of just... indifference felt like it might kill her.

"What is wrong with you?" She screamed, her voice breaking, tears streaming down her face. He stood there and just ...simply ...shrugged.

"It's not like you've given me any attention recently, is it, Em?" He asked, emotionlessly. She felt like she'd been kicked in the throat.

“I was sick.” She choked out, and Jon laughed bitterly.

“In the entire time I’ve known you, Emma, you’ve never not been sick.” His voice cut her in ways she never realised she could be cut, and she felt herself stagger backwards. She felt Holly’s strong hands grip her arms, and let herself be led away, not even caring where they were going. Her arms came up around herself, almost in a comforting gesture, like she was hugging herself, and felt that mole, rounded and domed.

***

An hour later, Emma found herself on her sofa, cup of tea in hand, staring at the breakup text that had just been sent. Holly had had to send it, because Emma’s hands had been too shaky, but since then Emma hadn’t been able to do anything. Holly was buzzing around the house, grabbing anything of Jon’s she could find and dumping them in bin bags, but Emma felt like she was glued to the sofa, melting into it. She stared at the read notification as her hand found that mole, that damn mole, yet again.

Chapter Eleven

Emma watched the two women through the crack in the door. She dared not move in case the floor squeaked, or breathe, in case they could hear her. It was close to the end now. She knew it. Lisa knew it. And Annette knew it.

They were all taking it differently. Emma couldn't let her mum go. Annette was more than ready, and Lisa just seemed to want to let her friend go in peace. But Emma couldn't understand why. Why wouldn't they want to fight? Why would they just let her go? It wasn't fair.

Emma shifted her weight onto her other leg and the floorboard squeaked loudly. Hand over her mouth, she tried not to make any more noise, hoping they hadn't heard her, but she knew she had been discovered. She watched as Lisa stroked her mother's headscarf and turned away too late to make her escape.

"Young lady." She heard in a stern whisper behind her. She didn't even need to turn around before a strong, vice like grip grabbed her upper arm and dragged her away upstairs, almost throwing her down onto her own bed several rooms away. Annette had kept this room exactly how it had been before Emma moved out at eighteen: teal walls, peeling posters on the walls, edgy black furniture. She hated it. Emma could already feel her cheeks blaring scarlet. She had often been on the end of one of Lisa's lectures, and as a former headteacher, she knew Lisa knew how to give them.

"What are you doing?" Lisa hissed at her, and Emma found herself recoiling.

"I don't know what you mean." Emma couldn't look her in the eye. She felt like a naughty schoolchild.

"Your mother is in her last days. She needs to be surrounded by love and support and good wishes, not you walking around with a face like a slapped arse! She deserves to leave this life feeling accomplished and happy and that she made a difference here, not like she is a burden and an inconvenience to you!" Lisa continued. Emma's eyes stung with tears.

"It's not fair." She muttered underneath her breath.

"Well of course it's not fair, Emma! None of this is fair! Life isn't fair!" Lisa snapped. One stubborn tear escaped from Emma's eye and trickled traitorously down her cheek. Emma couldn't bear to look at her, but she heard Lisa's aggravated sigh.

"I know that this is very difficult for you, and I'm sorry for that. If I could take it away from you then I would, but I can't. And your mother needs you now, Emma." Lisa's voice softened as she stroked Emma's hair, but Emma pulled away, suddenly enraged.

"This isn't how it's supposed to be! I'm not supposed to look after her, it's supposed to be the other way around!" She shouted in a whisper, terrified that her mother may hear her. She couldn't let her down, not now. Finally, she met Lisa's gaze, full of irritation and grief and pity.

"That's the inevitable trick of aging, Emma. We end up switching at the end. They care for you at the beginning of your life, and you must care for them at the end." A deep sigh made its way out of Lisa, and she seemed to deflate slightly as she stood up, smoothing down her still pristine skirt.

"I'll say goodbye to Annette and then let myself out. Think about what I've said, Emma." Lisa stalked out of the room, leaving Emma alone to hear the click-clack of Lisa's retreating high heels.

Chapter Twelve

The mole was bigger. She knew it.

Emma stared intently at it. She was sure of it, sure that it had grown ever so fractionally, so fractionally that no one else could see it but her. But she knew.

She should have measured it. Why didn't she measure it? Then she would have proof to show people, and they could see exactly what she would see. Should she start measuring it now? Leave it a few days, have some evidence to show the doctor? But then she would have to leave it days, and with the already long waiting lists she could be waiting for weeks — months, even — and it would keep growing and growing and growing and making her sicker and sicker...

Or she could deal with it now.

That would be a terrible idea! She scolded herself at even the notion of it. *She had no medical knowledge, she should wait for a professional to look at it... but that could take weeks. And she had nursed her mother in her last months, and she loved those reality A&E paramedic shows so... really, she had some experience. And the peace of mind would be worth it. Yes. She just had to do it. It would be worth it.*

In a sort of daze, Emma walked into the bathroom, picking up her small, sharp scissors out of her first aid kit and holding them to her arms. Head spinning, sweat on her brow, hands shaking, she exhaled as carefully, slowly, she opened the blades and closed them around her skin. It bled more than she expected, and at the sight of the scarlet liquid her head started to spin. But she knew, she had to keep going. She continued, clipping at more and more of the skin, more and more blood seeping from the wound. It hurt more than she thought it would, but after a couple of moments it was done. She stared at the mole on the floor, nauseous but triumphant, grabbing a bandage out of her first aid kit.

Chapter Thirteen

This restaurant was not the type of place Emma would frequent. It was beautiful, that was sure; an expansive orangery themed building with ornate floor length Art Deco and small, decorative orange trees dotted around the room. The chairs were highbacked and covered in an emerald velvet material, and as Emma looked around she saw people eating lobster, steak tartare, Dorset crab, all rich people foods she had never even contemplated ordering before in her life.

This was not the type of place she was supposed to be. She was not the type of person to be in a place like this. She was an imposter. Emma wished that she could disappear inside her clothes, turn into a liquid and evaporate or sink through the floor tiles, anything, literally anything than having to sit here and pretend, although Lisa couldn't see her distress. Why would she? This was Lisa's world.

Lisa. She'd finally reached out, but Emma couldn't work out why. *Maybe she'd heard about the cancer. Maybe she'd heard about Jon. Maybe she just felt bad after all this time.*

Emma absentmindedly rubbed at the bandage, hoping she wouldn't start the bleeding again.

Lisa sat opposite from her, completely oblivious to Emma's discomfort, casually sipping on her glass of rose. Emma had never heard of the brand before, so she guessed it must be expensive. She fit in effortlessly, like she had been born to be here. How she and her mother had even come across each other to be friends, Emma would never understand.

She realised that Lisa was staring at her and tried to bring herself back to the conversation.

"Are you okay there?" Lisa asked, relaxed in her chair, eyebrow raised. Feeling even more out of place on this uncomfortable chair, Emma squirmed.

"I'm just not used to this kind of place." She admitted. *How could anyone be used to this kind of place?* Lisa chuckled.

"Well, your mother and I always had differing tastes." She chortled to herself, but seeing that Emma did not see the joke, her laugh just trailed off.

"How have you been, Emma? I heard that you were getting a mastectomy. I trust that went well. I'm sorry I wasn't there." Lisa smiled at her, but it didn't seem to reach her eyes.

"You didn't come and see me after." Emma muttered, thinking Lisa couldn't hear her, and watched as Lisa rolled her eyes.

"I know. I wanted to but I didn't think I would be received well, not after the last time I saw you." Lisa stated, a brief hint of apology in her voice.

"You're meant to be my aunt." Emma whined, feeling stupid as she heard the words come out of her mouth, and Lisa seemed to wince also.

"I know. I am sorry, Emma." Lisa leant over to squeeze Emma's hand, but Emma felt frozen. It was like she couldn't physically open her hand to squeeze Lisa's back, but she hoped that Lisa knew she wanted to. Lisa was the closest thing she had to an aunt, the last person who knew her mother. All she wanted was for Lisa to open her arms and to accept her fully, but she couldn't ask for that, of course, and anyways, she didn't know if Lisa would ever do that.

"I know." Were the words that Emma heard come out of her mouth, and she watched as Lisa's face fell. Lisa retracted her hand, touched up her hair, and picked up the menu again.

"How is Jonathan?" She asked, her tone decidedly colder. Emma tried not to think about how much the tone change hurt. *So, she didn't know about Jon. It was the cancer.*

"We're not together anymore." She replied, trying to make her voice as cold as Lisa's.

"That is a shame. What did he do?" Lisa asked nonchalantly. Immediately, Emma felt a spark of irritation.

"Why do you assume he did something?" She snapped, trying to keep the tone of her voice level. Lisa, still looking at the menu, shrugged her shoulders.

"I've known men like that my entire life. The way he was sniffing around the waitress that day... it was a matter of time, darling." The familiar pet name hurt Emma, but she tried not to let it show on her face. She decided not to say anything, but Lisa locked eyes with her.

"What did he do?" She asked again, her voice softer this time. Emma felt her bottom lip wobble.

"He got with a friend of mine. Gemma. You met her once." Emma's voice was small and pitiful, she thought to herself, and she watched as Lisa's face screwed up in anger before quickly smoothing itself out to a casual nonchalance, once again.

"Well, I never liked her." Lisa leant forward to squeeze Emma's hand yet again, withdrawing before she could be rejected. "She obviously couldn't have been a good friend." Lisa's eyes met Emma's and she smiled softly. But the moment was just that, a moment, and Lisa cleared her throat, picking up the menu again.

"Now! We must order something before they chuck us out. What do you want, Emma? Order anything you want, it's my treat." Lisa trilled. Emma chuckled.

"So, I can get the lobster?" She joked, and Lisa's face lit up.

"Shall we be naughty?" Lisa's eyes sparkled as she called over the waiter.

Chapter Fourteen

Emma awoke the next day with a toothache.

She wasn't entirely surprised. She hadn't known how to eat the lobster and had inadvertently tried to eat part of the shell, and even after that debacle, Lisa had insisted on ordering the largest slice of toffee apple ginger cake, which was decorated with large, sharp shards of cinder toffee. In a way, she was surprised she'd gotten away with just that. Emma had come home stuffed to the gills, feeling slightly nauseous from all the rich food she had eaten, and had immediately fallen asleep on the sofa.

And now she was pushing herself off of the sofa, joints cracking painfully after hours of no movement, still feeling overfull, and her tooth ached. Maybe there was some food caught behind it, or maybe it was just random pain, she thought. It would probably go by itself though.

***

This tooth pain was driving her insane. She couldn't sleep, could hardly drink. She didn't even try eating, thinking it was a lost cause. In a desperate attempt for any help, she quickly dialled her dentist's number. The wait for someone to pick up could only have been seconds, but it felt like hours. Finally, someone picked up.

"Hello, Safe Smile Dental Practice, Natalie speaking." Crackled down the phone. Emma could almost have passed out with relief.

"Natalie! Hello! Please, I really need some help, I need an emergency appointment," Emma could hear herself begging.

"Okay, I'll see what we can do. Can I have your name and date of birth please?" Natalie chirped down the phone. She was disgustingly chipper, Emma thought to herself.

"Emma Susanna Rayburn. 19th September 1997." She replied quickly, hearing the click-clack of computer keys down the phone.

"And what exactly is the problem?" Natalie asked. Emma rolled her eyes.

"I have a toothache. It started this morning. It really hurts." Emma could hear how pathetic she sounded, but she didn't even care at this point.

"So, we've actually just had a serious emergency come in, so we don't have any emergency appointments today, I'm afraid. But I can get you in before we open tomorrow, at 8am? I'm so sorry, that's the best I can do." Natalie sounded apologetic, but Emma couldn't even comprehend what she was saying.

“Tomorrow? But I’m in pain now!” Emma didn’t mean to shout, but she did nevertheless.

“I’m very sorry, Miss Rayburn, but that’s the best I can do, I’m afraid.” Natalie reiterated. Her voice was hesitant, and Emma realised how nervous the poor girl must be.

“Sorry, I’m sorry, I didn’t mean to shout.” she apologised, but the damage was already done, and the apology sounded hollow. “Please book me in for the 8am, if you still can.” She wouldn’t have blamed her if the appointment had ‘suddenly been filled’, but she heard the click-clack of the keyboard keys again.

“That’s all booked for you, Miss Rayburn. 8am tomorrow with Dr Raj.” Natalie’s voice sounded robotic, but Emma hardly heard that over the relief.

“Thank you! ...so much, Natalie. I’m sorry again for shouting.” Emma said again, and she heard a smile come back to the other girl’s voice.

“That’s okay. You’re in pain, it’s understandable for emotions to be high. We’ll see you tomorrow, Miss Rayburn.” Natalie concluded. Emma smiled, even though the other girl couldn’t see her.

“See you tomorrow, Natalie.” The phone clicked dead, and Emma sighed a big sigh of relief. 8am. That was just eighteen hours away. Eighteen hours. She could survive eighteen hours. She threw herself down on the sofa, wondering whether she had enough painkillers to get her to the appointment.

She closed her eyes, hoping if she zoned out the flaring pain would hurt less, when she heard a tap tap tap, before the familiar sound of the key scraping in the lock.

"You alright?" Holly called out. Normally, Emma would be over the moon to see Holly, but she found herself rolling her eyes, unnaturally grumpy at the intrusion into her personal space.

"Just let yourself in." Emma muttered, louder than she realised. She didn't realise that Holly had heard her, and only realised once she saw the hurt in her best friend's eyes.

"Sorry, my tooth hurts." She explained as way of apology, and Holly rolled her eyes.

"You might be in pain, but don't have a go at me about it. I've done nothing wrong." Holly scolded. Emma bit her tongue, trying desperately to hold any snippy remark back. Holly was right. It wasn't her fault she was in pain.

"Did I say you've done anything wrong?" She asked, her voice venomous and spiteful. Internally, she groaned. That wasn't how she meant that to come out. Holly's eyes widened and filled with tears.

"Why are you so upset with me?" Holly asked, her voice breaking slightly.

"I just said, my tooth hurts." Emma tried to sound nonchalant as she turned away from Holly, feeling guiltier and guiltier as she looked at her.

"Well, go to the dentist then." Holly's voice sounded heavy and sullen.

"I've bloody tried that and I can't get in until tomorrow!" Emma snapped. Holly didn't answer, just spun around and ran off, presumably to the bathroom, Emma supposed. She didn't get why Holly was being so emotional about everything when this wasn't about her. This pain was driving her insane. She had to do something about it.

"I'm just gonna take it out." Emma shouted, looking around for the small tool kit her mother had owned. She had it somewhere... something like that was too useful to get rid of. If she remembered where she last put it...

The inkling of an idea came to Emma's mind, and she reached underneath the sofa, easily finding the tool kit. She was so glad she had decided to leave it in the last place her mum had, it was the only way she ever remembered where it was. Opening the tool kit, she saw was she was looking for; a small, topaz pair of pliers. Relief flooded through her body, and she went to put the pliers in her mouth when...

Holly pulled her arm away and threw the pliers away from them. Emma rolled her eyes, and went to speak, but Holly cut her off.

"What the hell do you think you're doing?! Do you realise how dangerous that is? How sick you could get? How much you could mess up? You are not a dentist! Just wait for your appointment tomorrow!" She screamed.

"I can't wait, I'm in too much pain!" Emma screamed back. She knew that she was being selfish now, but pain made you selfish, and she was in so, so, much pain. Holly stared at her emotionlessly for a second, then grabbed the bag Emma hadn't even seen her put down.

"Get in the car." She muttered, turning away from Emma.

Chapter Fifteen

Emma was pissed.

Holly had driven her to her dentist on the other side of town, in silence, and somehow had managed to wrangle an emergency appointment for her, she didn't know how, and had managed to get Emma in right away. Emma had tried to thank her, but Holly refused to speak to her, deciding instead to stay in the waiting area instead. Luckily for Emma's anxiety, the appointment had gone over in quite a blur, with the tooth being extracted quickly, even if she wasn't quite sure what had been wrong? But when she left, Holly was nowhere to be seen.

Mouth bundled with gauze, Emma made her way out to the car park to see Holly's red little Ford Fiesta still there. Grumpy, but thankfully with significantly less pain, Emma let herself into the car.

"I can't believe you left me in there by myself. You know that cost me over £280 just to get that sorted out? You could have waited for me." Emma complained, trying to stanch the drool escaping her mouth with her hand.

"I did wait for you. And now, I will drop you home, and we will discuss everything that has happened today another time. Do your seatbelt." Holly instructed, and Emma absentmindedly followed her instruction.

"Don't you want to stay?" Emma asked, realisation dawning on her. Holly wouldn't look at her.

"No. You won't be alone." Holly stated emotionlessly.

"Who's coming over?" Emma was feeling anxious. Who could it be? Not Gemma, or Jon, surely? Possibly Sammy, but she doubted it.

"Lisa is." Holly answered. Emma didn't react, just shuffled down in her seat, wishing that this albeit awkward car ride would continue forever.

***

Holly hadn't stopped when dropping Emma off, even after Emma told her about the pain that had just started in her side.

"There's always something with you, Emma!" She had huffed before chucking her out on the curb outside her house, leaving her facing the house alone. Emma could already tell that Lisa was inside the house, and she wanted nothing more than to walk away, but she knew that she had to face this head on. As she took a step towards the house, the front door open, and Emma saw Lisa there, disappointment written all over her face.

"Get inside." Lisa instructed, before walking back into the house. Arms holding herself, and trying not to think about the weird pain that had just started in her abdomen.

"I don't get why you're mad at me." Emma slurred, walking into the house. Lisa slammed the door behind her.

"Putting a pair of pliers in your mouth to do at home dentistry? That is so, incredibly dangerous, Emma, whatever were you thinking?" Lisa shouted. In this light, with her hair flared out behind her, she kind of looked like a harpy, Emma thought, before feeling incredibly guilty. *That wasn't nice*, she thought to herself.

"It needed to come out." Emma argued back, although it sounded stupid as she said it.

"You had an appointment! Did the idea of taking painkillers not occur to you?" Lisa pressed, furious.

"Some things are too much for painkillers. Like I've got this pain in my side—" Emma started, but Lisa cut her off.

"Stop it, Emma! You need to grow up, and get over this little anxiety thing. We all have our troubles but we all must carry on. Your mother would be so disappointed in you." Lisa's words hung in the air between them, and Emma felt as if all the air had been sucked out of her chest.

"You should leave." She spluttered out, before turning and running into the downstairs bathroom, desperately holding her tears in, only letting them out once she heard the front door slam.

Chapter Sixteen

It was midnight, and Emma was still staring at her alarm clock. She had to get to sleep soon, she knew it. She was fortunate enough that her boss let her work remotely from home, but that didn't mean that he'd be lenient if she was late. But something was just ...wrong. She couldn't put her finger on what it was, just that there was something ...off in the atmosphere. She hated to think what it could be. Letting out a deep breath, Emma settled down, turned onto her side and closed her eyes.

"Emma!" It was the faintest cry, but Emma heard it immediately. It was different to how her mother had ever called her before; this cry was full of love and pain and panic, looking out for support, for someone to hold her hand. And although that cry filled Emma with terror, she bolted down the stairs, to her mum. She knew what this was, and she knew that Annette knew what this was, and she could not miss it. She ran as fast as she physically could, skidding to a halt in front of her mother.

The sight of her took her breath away. Annette's skin was almost grey pale. She had forgone her usual brightly coloured headscarves, and so she seemed to be blending into the brilliant white sheets. A single tear rolled down her face, and she held her hand out to Emma. Emma took her mum's hand immediately, kneeling next to her.

"I think it's time." Annette breathed. Unable to speak, Emma nodded. There was a giant lump in her throat, and she tried to swallow it down.

"And that's okay. It's okay if you need to go." She tried to smile, to look encouraging, but she was sure all her mum saw was a grimace. Annette was crying too, her other hand shakily raising to stroke Emma's face.

"I have to stay for you, to protect you." She whispered, her voice barely a crack. It must have been painful to force the words through her intensely cracked, dry lips, Emma thought.

"No, no you don't. You've done such a great job, but it's okay. It's time to rest now." Emma cooed to her mother, lying through her teeth. She hoped her mum didn't know she was lying.

"You're lying." Annette whispered, crying. Emma shook her head.

"It's okay, Mama, it's okay. I love you. I love you." Emma repeated. Annette continued to stroke her face, every breath getting heavier and heavier.

"I love you too honey." She replied for the last time, almost inaudible, breathlessly. Her chest stilled, her head moved back, the soft, loving light behind her eyes dimmed until it was entirely extinguished. Sudden panic flared through her, and Emma shook her, gently.

"Mama?" She cried, tears streaming down her face, already feeling how her mum's skin was cooling, how any trace of life has disintegrated from her body, how she was irrevocably and completely dead. She was alone.

Emma screamed.

Chapter Seventeen

Emma couldn't breathe.

She clawed at her throat, falling to the floor, trying desperately to dislodge whatever it was that felt wrapped around her neck, cutting off her air. She gasped and gasped, desperately trying to get any oxygen down her windpipe and into her lungs before she passed out. Her abdomen was throbbing, pain radiating throughout her body, and a broken cry managed to escape her mouth in between the gasps for air that wouldn't come.

She wanted to be home. She wanted to go home, and be safe, there with her mum, where her mum would wrap her in her arms and tell her everything would be alright everything was going to be alright she was safe here—

And the entire right side of her body HURT.

The pain crashed into her like waves, sapping her of strength, of the will to hold on even. Why wouldn't it stop? She needed it to be over. She needed it—

And then it dawned on her. There was only one reason why she would get a pain like this, a stabbing pain in the right-hand side of her torso. Her appendix! She had never had her appendix out — remembered even asking her mum if she should get it taken out pre-emptively — and now it had reared its ugly head to get her.

You can die from your appendix rupturing, Emma thought to herself. She had heard horror stories of people getting a strange pain in their tummy and keeling over dead hours later. In primary school there had been a boy whose appendix ruptured, and he ended up in the high dependency unit. And Emma's stomach had been hurting for hours now. It was too late for the hospital now; she wouldn't get there in time. But she couldn't just lie down and go, she had to do something. She had to do something. *She had to get it out.*

Emma tried to lift herself off of the floor, but the pain was getting worse and worse. Unable to stand to her full height, she stumbled into her small kitchen, grabbing random things she could get her hands on. A knife. Scissors. A handful of tea towels. She wasn't even necessarily sure what she was doing, but she watched herself as she lifted her vest, exposing the skin, and took the knife, driving it into the plain expanse of skin. She hissed at the pain but drive the knife deeper, throwing it across the room once she had made a big enough wound. Hands shaking, she took the scissors and started to cut the wound, making it wider and wider. The pain was overwhelming, and she felt like she might either pass out or throw up — or perhaps even both — but she had to keep going. She had to. She was nearly there.

The wound finally open enough, Emma plunged her hand inside. She didn't know what she was searching for, but she knew that she would know when she found it. Her hand gripped ...some kind of slippery organ, and the slight pressure made her head feel woozy and sent jolts of pain up and down her torso. The appendix felt hot and inflamed in her hand, and there was a slight vindication behind the pain. *She knew it.* She had known it.

Using all of her strength, Emma pulled... and ripped the appendix out, throwing it across the room. But the pain caught up with her, and her head rolled back, painfully hitting the tiled kitchen floor.

As she started to drift away from her body, and the darkness of unconsciousness crept in, she could have sworn she heard a key in the lock of her front door...

Chapter Eighteen

The funeral was on a Wednesday. It was the same day of the week her mum was born on, Emma noted, staring at the order of service.

Looking around, it didn't seem like there weren't many people there, Emma thought to herself. Lisa was sat next to her side, holding her hand, but when Emma looked around, she noticed that the chapel was half empty. She didn't understand it. Her mother had been a pillar in the community for years, organising fundraisers for the local schools, charity fun runs, afternoon teas for the elderly in the community. But all of that had stopped when she was diagnosed, and although people had visited her, the longer her illness when on, the more people became busy with their own lives, and the fewer visitors came. And now, at her last hurrah, so many of the faces in this room were faces Emma had not known long, faces of kindly nurses and cancer support group friends, and a few of Emma's friends there as well. *Where were all these people her mother had helped? Why had they all forsaken her in her time of need?*

Lisa's hand squeezed hers too tightly. Emma's head snapped back to the front, but every cell in her body was telling her to leave. Breathing out slowly, she tried to focus on the eulogy, but the elderly officiant just kept droning on and on, and Emma could feel her attention drifting again. Her eyes then focused on the coffin, the coffin that was larger than she thought it would be. Flowers were draped over it, pink carnations and red roses and the word MUM spelled out in flowers. A smaller flowered tribute lay underneath hers, spelling out ANNETTE in large yellow and orange blooms. The card attached read 'love, Lisa.' The sickly smell emanating from the flowers was overwhelming, and Emma had the strongest urge to vomit.

Her eyes watered as she stared at the casket. Her mother was in there. *How could her mother be in there? How could she be dead?* She could still almost hear her voice, smell her perfume, feel her presence all around her, while she herself just felt numb. How could it be then, that Annette Rayburn was dead, and that her hollowed out corpse of a daughter was still roaming the earth?

And suddenly the coffin was being lowered and Emma didn't even realise she had gotten up, walking towards the coffin, when her hand was being tugged and she found herself enveloped in arms she didn't recognise, and someone was stroking her hair and saying *"It's okay, sweetheart, it's okay,* but it never would be okay again because she was dead she was dead she was dead.

She didn't remember the rest of the funeral. She had vague recollections of Lisa guiding her to the car park, driving her home, and placing her on her living room sofa with a cup of tea, a sandwich and a kiss on the head as she told her to take care of herself. She didn't know how long she sat there for in the end, only when she eventually moved, the tea was cold, the sandwich was stale, and her joints screamed out in pain. She turned, hearing footsteps walk up to her door.

From where she was lying on the sofa, Emma could see a letter being pushed through the letter slot. *Ignore it,* she thought to herself. *It doesn't matter.* And she tried not to think about it, but she could see it there, just hanging there, as if the person who pushed it through the letterbox couldn't be bothered to finish their job. It hung there, taunting her, stark white against a dark mahogany wood door, and Emma stared at it and stared at it until...

She abruptly got up, head spinning at how fast she had moved after being sedentary so long, and stormed over to the door. Ripping the letter open, Emma's eyes scanned the words, taking in every single word on the paper, before dropping the letter.

"Where's my phone?" Emma muttered herself, recalling the words of the letter to herself as anxiety rose up her throat, threatening to choke her.

Chapter Nineteen

She smelt the hospital before she saw it, that all too familiar smell of antiseptic and disinfectant. Her heart sunk the second she smelt it, and she almost didn't want to open her eyes. Who knew what damage had been done to her body for her to wake up here? The longer it took for her to confront this, the better.

She tried to breathe evenly, her windpipe shaking slightly as she tried to continue. Already she felt overwhelmed; the incessant beeping of the machines surrounding her, the faint pressure of the needles inserted in her veins, the tingling of limbs that hadn't moved in days. Her throat seemed to tighten up, and she forced herself to inhale, exhale, inhale, exhale. But still, the panic rose up her throat, and she let out a little whimper of fear when she felt a soft, familiar hand land on hers.

"Lisa! Lisa, I think she's awake!" Holly's excitable whisper was the best thing Emma had ever heard. It felt like her chest might cave in with the relief. Still anxious, Emma started opening her eyes, squinting at the brightness of the hospital lights and Holly's smile.

"She is, Lisa! Hey, Emma!" Holly was almost buzzing, and Emma found herself blinking slowly to try and reorient herself.

"What are you doing here?" She asked, her voice thick and slow. Holly smiled sweetly down at her.

"We weren't going to just leave you here on your own, now, were we?" She whispered, carefully leaning down to give Emma a cuddle. "Just have to be careful, they had to make more of an incision than they hoped."

"But why are you here? We argued." Emma's voice was slurred and she tried to sit up, but her abdomen seemed to scream in pain. She gasped, leaning forward in an attempt to stop the pain, and felt a large, fluffy cushion be placed behind her.

"We're family, Emma. Of course we would be here, darling." Lisa smiled at her, stroking Emma's hair absentmindedly as she sat next to her on the bed, Holly crawling on as well. Emma felt tears leak from the corner of her eyes.

"I'm sorry." She choked, trying to apologise to both of them at once, and they both enveloped her in their arms and love.

"I'm sorry, darling, I should have been more present with you." Lisa whispered.

"You don't have to apologise. I'm sorry I couldn't see how much pain you were in." Holly smiled.

"I was awful to you." Emma wailed, and was shushed by Lisa.

"Pain turns you into a different person. You needed help." Lisa murmured, wisely. "I think maybe we need to recognise that more."

"And maybe we need to look into different types of therapy, see if we can get you some help?" Holly asked, obviously worried at the question, but her tense body language released once Emma nodded.

"I think that's a good idea." Emma agreed.

"And I'm coming to stay with you for a bit. No arguments, it is happening. Can't have your mother coming to haunt me." Lisa raised her eyebrows jokingly as she smiled at Emma. "It's time for me to be a proper aunt." A tear fell down her cheek, which she hastily wiped away.

"Should we watch a movie or something while we wait for the doctor to come around? I hate hospitals." Holly asked, immediately grabbing her phone. "I wonder if I can cast to the hospital tv." Lisa gasped.

"We should watch that new nature documentary, Sloth Undercover, it looks just darling!" Emma snorted, watching Lisa's face light up.

"I don't think that's what you think it's gonna be." She laughed as Lisa pouted.

"I just saw a clip of someone giving a sloth a bath, it looked adorable! Well, let me look at the options then!" She reached over Emma to take Holly's phone, and for just a second, Emma genuinely believed that everything was going to be alright.

Epilogue

Dear Emma Susanna Rayburn,

We are writing to you to inform you that you may be a candidate for genetic testing. Our records show that your mother, Annette Rayburn, has developed diseases linked to the BRCA 1 and 2 genes. As these genes have been linked to inherited mutations, we advise you to speak to a healthcare professional. Finding out if you have an inherited mutation linked to the BRCA 1 and 2 genes can help reduce your risk for developing breast or ovarian cancers.

We hope you find this information useful.

Sincerely,

Dr Erin Kain

About The Author

About the Author

A traveller, film analyst and lover of stories, Sarah started writing in early childhood and has never looked back. Her 'first' story, The Toilet Monsters, got rave reviews from her six year old peers.

Before deciding to follow her writing dreams, Sarah got a degree in Film Studies from the University of Winchester and dabbled in screenwriting, before returning to literary fiction. Her first book, The Great European Escape: The Trials and Tribulations of Travelling While Chronically Ill was self published in July 2023, and her debut fiction novella, Amissis Liberis, was published by Alien Buddha Press in May 2024. She has also published extensively in literary magazines and in anthologies Broken Olive Branches, edited by Stephanie Rabig and There's Nothing Out There by Black Shuck Books.

Sarah lives in the U.K., but frequently travels internationally. She has read for Aurealis and HerStry, and has also been a fiction editor for the Candid Review. She specialises primarily in horror or fiction with horrific elements, but also writes speculative fiction and film analysis.

Sarah can be found on Twitter/X, Instagram, Bluesky, Substack and TikTok under the username aldbera, or on her website sarahrnew.wordpress.com.

Also by Sarah R. New

The Great European Escape (2023)
Amissis Liberis (2024)

Coming Soon

Coming soon...CATFOOD

Pina loves Elias, and she'll do anything to save him. When kitten Pina's human Elias is hospitalised after a fight with his partner Tommy, Pina and her fellow cats Artichoke and Biscuit decide to scare Tommy away. But something goes horribly wrong...

CATFOOD is a graphic horror-thriller that explores the devotion between a man and his feline family.

www.ingramcontent.com/pod-product-compliance
Ingram Content Group UK Ltd.
Pitfield, Milton Keynes, MK11 3LW, UK
UKHW011502170226
10751UKWH00002B/227